ISBN: 0-439-69627-5

Madagascar TM & © 2005 DreamWorks Animation L.L.C.

Published by Scholastic Inc.
SCHOLASTIC and associated logos are trademarks
and/or registered trademarks of Scholastic Inc.

12 11 10 9 8 7 6 5 4 3 2 1   5 6 7 8 9 10/0

Designed by Joseph Williams
Printed in the U.S.A.
First printing, May 2005

MADAGASCAR™

MOVIE STORYBOOK

Adaptation by Billy Frolick
Illustration by Koelsch Studios

DREAMWORKS
ANIMATION SKG

SCHOLASTIC INC.

New York   Toronto   London   Auckland   Sydney
Mexico City   New Delhi   Hong Kong   Buenos Aires

A DAY AT THE ZOO

People began to pour through the zoo gates, hurrying to see their favorite animals.

The star of the show, Alex the lion, climbed onto a fake rock and struck a majestic pose.

"It's showtime!" Marty the zebra said. He moonwalked and made armpit noises. Now for the big finish! He took a mouthful of water and sprayed the crowd like a firehose. The children loved it, but the adults weren't so thrilled.

After the crowd had left, Marty was bored. And a little let down. Was anything exciting ever going to happen? Suddenly four penguins popped up in his pen. They were holding spoons, which they were using to dig a tunnel.

"What continent is this?" asked Skipper, the penguins' leader.

"Manhattan," Marty said.

"We're still in New York. Abort! Dive! Dive! Dive!" cried Skipper, and all the penguins disappeared back down the hole.

"Wait!" Marty cried. "What are you guys doing?"

"We're going to the wide-open spaces of Antarctica. To the wild!" Skipper said, sticking his head back out of the hole.

"The wild? You can actually go there?" Marty asked.

But the penguins were gone.

That night, Alex, Gloria the hippo, and Melman the giraffe had a birthday party for Marty. There were presents and a cake.

"Make a wish," said Gloria. Marty thought for a few seconds, then blew out the candles.

"C'mon, what'd ya wish for?" Alex asked.

"I wished I could go to the wild!" Marty announced.

"But it's unsanitary!" said Melman. He hated germs.

"Doesn't it bother you that you don't know anything about life outside this zoo?" Marty asked.

"Nope," was the unanimous reply.

"The food, the fans, the pampering," said Alex. "It really doesn't get any better. Even the star is out."

"Helicopter," Marty said as the "star" flew off.

"Buddy, listen," Alex said. "Everyone has days when they think the grass might be greener somewhere else."

"Come on," Marty replied, looking at his jungle mural with curiosity. "I just feel there's gotta be more to being a zebra than this."

"You're my best friend. Are you going to just give that up?" Alex went to get some sleep. But Marty stood in his enclosure, staring at his mural.

"Alex. Alex! It's Marty!" Melman cried. "He's gone."

"Where would he go?" asked Gloria.

"The wild," Alex replied. "If the people find out, they're going to be mad. We gotta go after him."

Now the three friends were really worried. They had to find Marty. They decided to go to the train station to look for him.

Meanwhile, Marty was enjoying all that Manhattan had to offer — strutting the streets, talking to a police horse in Times Square, even ice-skating! At last, he was on his way to the wild.

Alex, Gloria, and Melman decided to take the subway
to the train station. The people on the subway had never
seen zoo animals outside of the zoo before. They kept
getting off the train as quickly as they could. But the
three friends didn't notice — they were only thinking
about finding Marty.

By the time Alex, Melman, and Gloria finally caught up with Marty at Grand Central Station, people were screaming and running everywhere. One brave old lady even attacked Alex as he ran toward Marty.

"Do you realize what you put us through?" asked Alex, shaking Marty. "Don't you ever, ever do this again!"

Suddenly there was a rumble. Slowly the animals turned around. Masses of policemen in riot gear swarmed the hall. Alex tried to explain, but it was too late.

A dart hit Alex on the leg and before he could do anything he fell asleep.

In another part of the hall, the penguins had also realized that the jig was up.

"Cute and cuddly, boys," Skipper ordered his troops. "Cute and cuddly."

The four friends woke up in wooden crates on a ship bound for Africa.

"It's a zoo transfer!" groaned Alex.

"Calm down," Marty cried. "Take it easy. We are going to be o-kizzay."

"No, Marty! We are not going to be o-kizzay. This is all your fault!" Alex shouted.

He and Marty began shoving at the walls of their crates, trying to push the other's over. All the crates began to rock back and forth.

Gloria asked, "Does anyone feel sick?"

"I feel sick," Melman moaned.

"Melman, you *always* feel sick," said Alex.

The penguins were also on the ship. Rico stuck his head out of an airhole and began to pick the lock on their crate. Soon the penguins were free.

The penguins decided to take over the ship. They tied up the captain, and then Skipper and his crew tried to figure out how to steer the ship.

"Status!" Skipper demanded.

"I don't know the codes," said Private.

"Don't give me excuses," Skipper barked. "Give me results! Let's get this tin can turned around!"

Three penguins jumped on the ship's wheel, and the huge ship slowly began to make a tight turn.

Up on deck, the rocking crates had broken loose from their ties. As the ship turned, they began to slide across the deck. They moved faster and faster . . . until they hit the railing and stopped. Then Gloria's crate crashed into the other three. The railing snapped, and all four crates flew overboard.

THE WILD

The crates floated and bobbed on the waves until they finally washed up on shore. Alex, Gloria, Melman, and Marty were all back together. But where were they?

"San Diego," Melman announced. The others turned to stare at him. "White, sandy beaches, wide-open enclosures. This could be the San Diego Zoo."

"San Diego! What could be worse than San Diego?" Alex moaned.

But Marty liked what he saw. "This place is crack-a-lackin'!" he cried.

Gloria grabbed Alex before he could start chasing Marty and hung on tight. "We're just going to find the people," she said soothingly, "and get this mess straightened out!"

Alex heard music. The four friends followed the sound into the jungle. A group of lemurs were dancing wildly around a huge tree.

"It's not people. It's animals!" Gloria exclaimed. "What kind of zoo is this?"

"I'm liking San Diego! This place is fresh!" Marty said, getting into the groove.

No one noticed another group of mean-looking locals, the fossa, watching the dancers . . . and drooling hungrily.

The fossa pounced. All of the cute lemurs ran away — all except one. The fossa surrounded him and threw him into a salad bowl. Alex burst into the clearing.

A huge spider landed on his shoulder. "Aaaagh! Aaaaaagh!" he cried as he danced around, trying to shake it off.

The fossa panicked at the sight of the crazed lion and melted back into the jungle.

Gloria picked up Mort, the cute little lemur, and cuddled him. "Did the big, bad putty tat scare you?" she asked. Mort cooed at her.

Suddenly another lemur, Maurice, emerged from the jungle. He cleared his throat. "Presenting, Your Royal Highness, King Julien the thirteenth!"

Julien marched out of the bushes.

"He's got style," Marty whispered.

"What is he? A guinea pig?" Alex asked.

"Welcome," Julien said. "Welcome to the wild. We thank you with enormous gratitude for chasing away the fossa."

"The wild?" Alex shouted in disbelief.

Marty's birthday wish had come true — he was in the wild!

"We're in the wild! We're in the wild!" he yelled gleefully, dancing around the beach. "This could be the best thing that's ever happened to us!"

Alex didn't think so. In fact, he was sure that it was the worst thing that had ever, *ever* happened to him. All he could do was hope for a rescue boat.

Back on the ship, the penguins celebrated as they headed toward Antarctica. "Well, boys," Skipper exclaimed, "it's gonna be ice-cold sushi for breakfast!" The penguins high-fived and settled down to some serious partying.

Alex had had it with Marty. Alex prowled down the beach and drew a line in the sand. "I've had enough of this! This is your side of the island and this is our side of the island, for those who love New York and care about going home."

"Fine," said Marty. "You all have your side, and I have mine. If you need me, I'll be over here, on the fun side of the island."

Gloria was posing with her arm in the air while Alex built a giant statue. "When the moment is right, we will ignite the beacon of liberty," he explained, putting the finishing touches on the rescue beacon.

Melman rolled his eyes but kept on rubbing two sticks together to start a fire. "Why can't we borrow some of Marty's fire?" he asked, glancing over to the "wild" side of the island where Marty was sitting beside a campfire.

"That's 'wild' fire. We're not using 'wild' fire on Lady Liberty," Alex replied.

Suddenly Melman's sticks caught fire . . . frightening Melman. He staggered toward the statue, which burst into flames and collapsed.

"Can we go to the fun side now?" Melman asked.

Finally Alex gave in and went over to the fun side of
the island. Gloria and Melman were already there, staying
with Marty in his cozy hut.

"I've been kind of a jerk," Alex said to Marty. "If this is
what you want, then I'll give it a shot."

"Welcome to *Casa del Wild*," smiled Marty.

Together again, the four friends spent the rest of the evening eating seaweed kabobs and stargazing.

The only thing that was missing was Alex's favorite food. Suddenly he couldn't stop dreaming about steak. It was very strange.

The lemurs gathered to discuss the new arrivals.

"For as long as we can remember, we have been attacked and eaten," Julien said. "We will make the New York giants our friends. With Mr. Alex protecting us, we'll be safe and never have to worry about the dreaded fossa ever again!"

"Yay!" the lemurs shouted.

"I have a plan. The New York giants will wake up in paradise!" Julien yelled.

Meanwhile, the penguins had finally reached Antarctica — and they didn't like it. It was cold . . . very cold. So they headed back to the ship to look for someplace warm.

"Welcome to paradise!" Julien announced the next morning as the four friends gathered for a breakfast of fruits and vegetables — all supplied by the lemurs.

Alex, Marty, Gloria, and Melman looked around in amazement. They were standing in front of Marty's mural at the zoo . . . only this was real!

"How about once around the park?" Marty asked. "Who's with me?"

Alex suddenly took off running, with Marty in hot pursuit. The pair ran through the wild, tackling each other and having fun. But something strange was happening to Alex. By the time they returned to the waterhole, Alex was feeling better — and wilder — than he'd ever felt before.

After breakfast, Marty introduced Alex for a show
unlike any he had ever performed in the New York zoo.
"Ladies and gentlemen. Primates of all ages. The wild
proudly presents the king . . . Alex the lion!"

Alex leaped onto a rock
and, for the first time in
his life, really
ROARED!

"Whoa," said Gloria. "I
never heard that before."
    The locals began
cheering and doing the wave. Alex threw his arms in the
air. . . . *Shing!* . . . Claws popped out of his paws.

Alex's act was better than anything he'd ever done at the zoo, but he couldn't stop smelling steak. And it was making him really hungry. He opened his mouth to let out another roar, but bit Marty instead.

Alex's new act was no *act*. Living in the wild was making his behavior . . . wild!

There was only one thing to do.

"Your friend is what you'd call a deluxe model hunting-and-eating machine," Julien explained. "Mr. Alex belongs with his own kind, on the fossa side of the island."

Everyone stared at Alex, who began to back away into the jungle until he disappeared.

Marty was confused. "This isn't how the wild is supposed to be. . . ." he said as he stared after his friend.

"We're a team, we'll figure this out," Gloria said.

Braaaap!

"Gloria!" Melman scolded.

"That was not me, okay. That was the boat. The boat!"

"Come on . . . we gotta flag it down!" said Marty.

The three friends ran down to the beach, waving and calling. The boat began to turn toward them.

"It's coming back! It's coming back!" Gloria screamed.

"You guys hold the boat. I'll go get Alex," Marty cried, running back toward the jungle.

An anchor thudded into the sand. The penguins slid down the chain and landed next to Gloria and Melman.

Marty finally found Alex, sleeping in a homemade lion hut.

"Alex! The boat is here! We can go home!"

"Stay away!" Alex said. "I'm a monster."

"No, you're not," replied Marty. "You're the best friend a guy could have, and I'm not leaving without you."

But Alex just went back into his hut.

While Marty and Alex had been talking, the fossa had been gathering. When Alex went back inside, they began to pour down from the rocks to surround the zebra.

Marty took one look at the hungry fossa and began running, and calling for Alex. But there were too many fossa. He was trapped.

A yell split the air. It was Melman swinging on a vine
like Tarzan. He grabbed Marty and carried him out of
the fossa ring. Gloria was waiting for them, and the three
friends took off running.

Just as the fossa were getting closer, Skipper and
his troops popped up. A fierce battle erupted with the
penguins, the lemurs, and the three friends fighting side
by side, but they were outnumbered.

Just when it looked like the fossa would win, a roar brought the fight to a sudden stop. Alex leaped into the brawl.

"It's showtime," he said, winking at his friends. Then he turned to face the fossa. "I never, ever want to see you on my turf again!" He roared at the terrified fossa, who didn't wait any longer. They turned and *ran* to the other side of the island.

That night, there was a huge party to celebrate. Music played, and the penguins made sushi. Alex ate some. It wasn't steak, but he liked it a lot.

As the four friends looked around at the locals and the penguins, they realized that it didn't matter where they were as long as they were together. Marty's dream of living in the wild had come true. And he and Alex were friends again. Things couldn't get any better. With that they all raised their coconut cups in a toast.